This book is
fondly dedicated
to my children,
Judy and Jim

Library of Congress Cataloging in Publication Data
Smath, Jerry.   The housekeeper's dog.
SUMMARY: A dog who likes to roll, scratch,
and play with bones is quite a different dog after
attending Madame De Poochio's School for Dogs.
[1. Dogs—Fiction]   I. Title.
PZ7.S6393Ho   [E]   80–10580
ISBN 0–8193–1023–9   ISBN 0–8193–1024–7 lib. bdg.

The Housekeeper's Dog

by
Jerry Smath

Parents Magazine Press • New York

In a big house, on an elegant street,
lived a very rich man and his very rich wife.
They were very, very tidy.
If the least little thing was dirty,
they were upset.

So every day Miss Dilly,
the housekeeper, came in to clean.

Every night Miss Dilly
went home to her own little house.
And every night her dog
greeted her at the door.

The housekeeper loved her dog very much.

She loved to watch him roll ...

and scratch ...

and play with his bone.

One day, Miss Dilly brought
her dog to the big house.
She was going on her vacation trip.

"May I leave my dog with you
while I'm gone?" she asked the
very rich man and his very rich wife.

Just then the dog started to scratch.
They looked at him with horror.
The very rich man said,
"I know a place where your dog
can have a vacation, too.
In fact, he will come back a new dog."

The housekeeper was pleased that
her dog would also have a vacation.
So she left on her trip,
and the very rich man took her dog to
Madame De Poochio's School for Dogs.

"I see you have a messy dog,"
said Madame De Poochio.

"Yes, indeed," said the rich man.
"He does nothing but roll
and scratch and play with his bone."

"I shall fix that,"
said Madame De Poochio.
"Come back in two weeks.
He will be a new dog by then."

When the housekeeper's vacation
was over, she stopped at the big house.
"Where is my dear dog?" she asked.
"I've missed him very much."

The rich lady rang for her butler.
"Please ask the housekeeper's dog
to join us," she said.

At first Miss Dilly
didn't recognize her dog.
Then she ran to give him a big hug.

The housekeeper was shocked
to hear her dog talk.
And she couldn't believe the way he looked.
"You've changed," she said.
"Come, we're going home to
our own little house."

Once outside, the dog said,
"The sun is hot today.
Please open your umbrella
so I may stay cool."

"Of course, dear dog,"
said the housekeeper.

Then the dog said,
"This sidewalk is very dirty.
Please call a taxi."

Miss Dilly didn't have much money.
But she wanted to please her dog.
So she said, "Of course, dear dog,"
and called a taxi.

"Home at last!" said Miss Dilly.
"Now you can roll and scratch
and play with your bone."

"Roll? Scratch? Play with my bone?
Certainly not!" said the dog.
"I might get dirty. But I am hungry.
Please prepare my dinner."

"Of course, dear dog," said the housekeeper.

She opened a can of his favorite dog food.
"Dog food!" said the dog.
"I want to eat what you eat.
And I want to sit at the table."

"Of course, dear dog," said the housekeeper.

"You must be tired," she said.
"I will put a fresh blanket in your box."

"My old box is much too small," said the dog.
"I prefer a bed in a room of my own."

There was only one bedroom in the house.
So Miss Dilly said, "Very well, take mine."

That night the dog
slept soundly
in the big bed ...

while the housekeeper tossed and turned
on the couch.

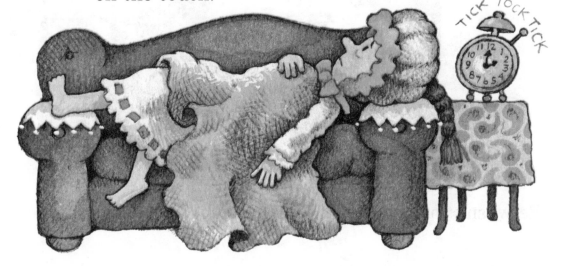

TICK TOCK TICK

The next day at work she was very tired.
So she returned home early.
"My dog will cheer me up," she thought.
But he was nowhere in sight.

He wasn't in the kitchen.   He wasn't in the living room.

He wasn't in the closet.
And he wasn't in the cellar.

Miss Dilly was afraid.
"Something terrible must have
happened to my dog!" she screamed.

Just then she heard a sound
coming from the bedroom.

Slowly, she opened the door
and there was her dog,
stretching and yawning.
"Dear me, I must have
slept all day," said the dog.
"Bring me breakfast in bed.
I would like bacon and eggs,
toast, and a large glass of milk."

The housekeeper was so happy
to find her dog
that all she could say was,
"Of course, dear dog."
And she brought him breakfast in bed.

Next morning, a letter arrived
for the housekeeper's dog.
"I've been invited to a costume party at
Madame De Poochio's School for Dogs," he said.
"Give me money to buy a costume!" he demanded.

The dog took the money and left
without even saying thank you ...
and bought the most expensive
costume he could find.

It was an elegant party.
Dogs from all over town were there.

And not one of them rolled,
scratched, or played with a bone.

When the party was over,
the housekeeper's dog said,
"I live in a small house
but I have my own housekeeper.
Come and live with me and we will
have parties like this every day."
So they all followed the dog
to the housekeeper's house.

Miss Dilly was still at work.
All the dogs walked right in
and made themselves at home.

When she returned home
and saw all the dogs,
she became angry.
"You are a selfish, selfish dog,"
she shouted.

"How dare you talk to me like that!"
replied her dog.
"Come, we're leaving," he said to his friends.
"This house is too small anyway.
I'll take you to a house much bigger
and much more elegant than this one."

He took them to the big house
where the very rich man
and the very rich woman lived.
He led the other dogs right in
without even knocking.

KEEP OFF
THE
GRASS

WIPE
YOUR
FEET

Their noise woke the man and his wife,
who were asleep upstairs.
"Get those untidy beasts out of here!"
screamed the lady.
The man called the dog catcher
and then raced downstairs to
grab the housekeeper's dog.

All the dogs were running away
just as the dog catcher arrived.
"Help me!" cried the housekeeper's dog.
But his friends just kept running.

So he ran too ...

till he reached the little house.
"Stop!" yelled Miss Dilly.
"Let go of my dog at once."

"How do I know this is your dog?"
asked the dog catcher.

"My dog likes to roll and scratch
and play with his bone," she replied.
"Let him go, and see for yourself."

So the dog catcher let go of the dog.

He rolled ...

and scratched ...

and played with his bone.

The dog catcher smiled.
It was enough proof for him.

"Now come inside, dear dog," said Miss Dilly.
"For I've missed you very much."

ABOUT THE AUTHOR/ARTIST

After working in films for many years,
JERRY SMATH turned to illustration
for children's magazines and children's
textbooks. He made his first appearance
as an author/illustrator with But No
Elephants for Parents. For this, his
second book, he has created another
lively story with equally spirited pictures.

Jerry Smath lives in Westchester County,
New York. He has a dog who loves to
roll and scratch and play with a bone.